MY FIRST BOOK OF
RIDDLES

Story by Janet & Alex D'Amato
Illustrated by Kelly McMahon

Treasure Books™
a division of
PRICE STERN SLOAN
Los Angeles

ISBN 0-8431-4150-6

What do cats have that no other
animals have?

Kittens!

What animal keeps the best time?

A watchdog!

What are you when you have a cold?

A little horse!

How do you get fur from a tiger?

Run!

What three keys have legs, but won't open locks?

Monkeys! Donkeys! Turkeys!

What should a man know before trying
to teach tricks to a dog?

More than the dog!

What part of a fish weighs the most?

The scales!

What side of a cat has the most fur?

The outside!

If five elephants were chasing you,
what time would it be?

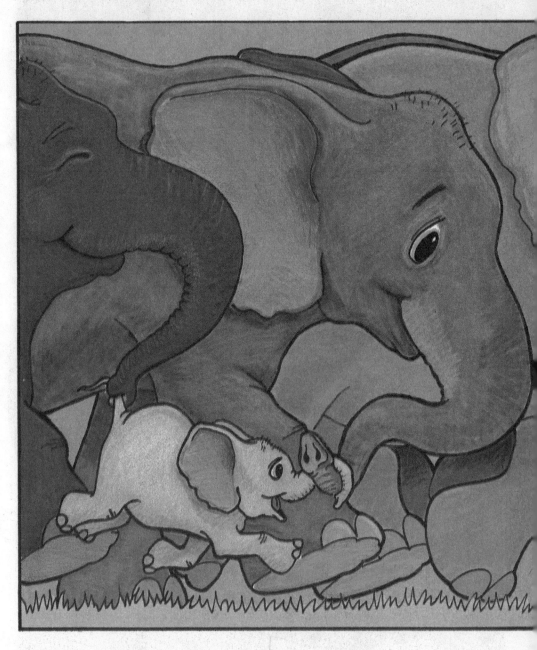

Five after one!

What would you have if you put three ducks in a box?

A box of quackers!

What's more wonderful than
a counting dog?

A spelling bee!

What's long, green and has sixteen wheels?

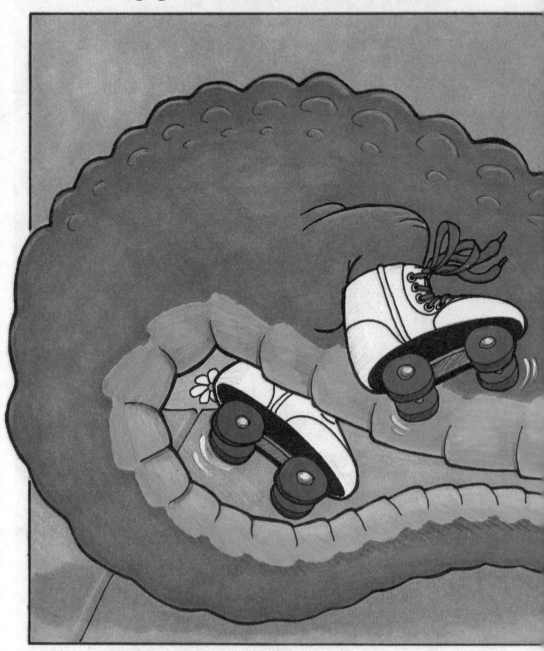

An alligator on rollerskates!

What does a giraffe become after one year?

A two-year old giraffe!

What do dogs and trees have in common?

Their bark!

What would you like to be on a cold day?

A little otter!

What's brown and white, has
four legs and a trunk?

A cow on vacation!

Why do birds fly south in the winter?

Because the train is too crowded!

What do you lose whenever you stand up?

Your lap!

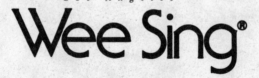